First published 1989 by
Walker Books Ltd
87 Vauxhall Walk,
London SE11 5HJ

2 4 6 8 10 9 7 5 3 1

© 1989 Nick Butterworth

Printed in Hong Kong

ISBN 0-7445-5127-7

MY GRANDPA IS AMAZING

Nick Butterworth

WALKER BOOKS
AND SUBSIDIARIES
LONDON • BOSTON • SYDNEY

My grandpa is amazing.

He builds fantastic
sand-castles…

and he makes
marvellous drinks…

and he's not at all
afraid of heights…

and he makes wonderful
flower arrangements…

and he's a brilliant
driver…

and he knows
all about first aid...

and he's got
an amazing bike…

and he's a terrific
dancer...

and he's very, very,
very patient…

and he invents
brilliant games.

It's great to have
a grandpa like mine.

He's amazing!